Monae & Renee

Love and Betrayal

Yanee Brinks

Contents

Chapter One

Monae

When we were ready to put our plan into motion it was too late. Someone had beaten us to the job. But who wanted him dead? We didn't know of any other people that had an issue with David.

The plot thickened as we all felt some type of way about this sudden shake up. Could we really trust that one of us hadn't done it and just wasn't being honest about it?

I stayed up all night thinking about it when we found out. It really rattled my nerves that I wasn't the one behind his murder. He had crossed the line and I wanted to get even.

Time went on and eventually we all grew to believe that we weren't the ones who offed him. Mario had an alibi and Renee was with me at home. So we moved past that and was now focused on our futures.

Renee was free to date Mario and I was free to be with Brandon. Yes, we are still together. Four years had really flew by but now I was legal. It was time to celebrate hard.

Renee had been in the deep friend zone with Mario for awhile but once she was legal he swooped in on her fast. He wasn't playing any games with her ass. I was all for it because he treated her like a queen so I knew she was in good hands.

Meanwhile me and Brandon had been together for what seemed like forever. I was still mad crazy about my baby and so was he. Now that I was legal he clung to me like I was going to run away or something.

But maybe he did think that I would venture off his trail. After all I had grown into my body too now and fully adapted to the girly changes that I had been making over the years.

I guess you could say that I was feeling myself a little bit but in no way was I going to leave him. He was still my rock. He had taught me so much since meeting him and we continued to learn together.

Today I had something important to ask him. I was nervous for some reason but I really wanted to put this in his head. So when I left my job interview I worked up the nerves to ask him.

"Babe I was thinking. We spend so much time together and you've helped me redecorate the house so much that why don't you move in with me." I said in a shy voice

"So you wanna play house, huh?" Said Brandon with a smirk

His sexy ass smirk instantly got me wet. Brandon had grown into his body too. His eyes were still hypnotizing brown. His hair was short and curly but his body was built and banging.

I got lost in his eyes and smirk as he started laughing.

"What? What's so funny?" I asked annoyed

"You. I bet you ain't heard a thing that I said have you?" He asked me laughing

"Honestly, no I didn't." I replied

"You a trip baby but I'll tell you this. I'll move in officially if GiGi says it's cool. I don't want to offend her. I love GiGi." He said as he leaned over and kissed me

"Really babe?!" I said with much enthusiasm

"Yes" He said

I was beaming inside. All I needed to do was win over GiGi. It's not like he hadn't been spending the night with me from time to time but those were special occasions as GiGi called them.

I wanted him by my side every night though. It was time for us to officially be "together". The whole trip home I just kept praying that her answer would be yes. I texted her before we got there saying that I needed to talk to her so hopefully she would be ready because I was.

We walked in the house and GiGi was there waiting and watching a television show with Renee. I walked in beaming with pride hoping that my good mood would rub off on them and win a yes from GiGi.

"So how was the interview sis?" Asked Renee

"It went good sis. I think I got the job." I replied

"Yea congrats big sis. I'm so proud of you!"

"Yeah cograts lil Miss Monae. You're all grown up now but you're still my little girl." GiGi said with a smile

"Thanks GiGi." I said flopping down next to her and hugging her

"GiGi I wanted to ask you though would it be okay if Brandon moved in with us. Its not a need but a want. I want him near me and since he does help out here a lot I just wanted him to live here with me." I pleaded with the saddest eyes that I could give her

She sat there staring at me like I had two heads. Then she gave Brandon the side eye.

"I told her the only way that I would do it is if you consent to it." He said throwing his hands up

She nodded then looked back at me. I was getting scared that she would say no. Just then she said it "I approve". I jumped in her lap and buried her in kisses. This was truly a good day for me.

"But with a live-in boyfriend comes more complications so be prepared." She whispered in my ear

I nodded and took heed of what she said. I'm sure that I would understand what she meant by that later. But for now, I was happy and ready to celebrate with my man.

But of course Renee wasn't ready for that to happen. She didn't say anything directly but she shot me a dirty look. I thought she would have been happy for me but I guess not.

Shit she was barely here anyway with her many nights at her new boyfriend house. He kept her on a close leash but so far he wasn't bat shit crazy. Not that I could see anyway.

I gave Brandon a kiss and headed down stairs hoping that Renee would follow me. She did and I was ready for her attitude.

"So that's what we're doing now? Just moving extra people into our quiet space without consulting each other." She said full of attitude

"Well considering your barely here with me anyway I didn't think that you would care. When was the last time that you were here with me?" I said causing her to change that look on her face

"So if anything was to happen while you were away having fun and getting your back blown out I'd be dead until you decided to come check. This way I can have some security here with me. Besides you never cared when he spent the night." I continued to say

Renee didn't say anything. She just turned away and walked back upstairs. I hated that she didn't apologize for her ignorance but I was happy that I shut her down.

When I got back upstairs Brandon was still there

talking to GiGi. They got along well now and I loved that. It was great because I considered Brandon family as well as GiGi.

Once I returned to the living room GiGi got up to congratulate us and left. That left just me and my babe. It was time to celebrate. I jumped in his arms and started kissing him.

Brandon laughed and said "I knew your ass couldn't wait for this."

"You know it. Now shut up and fuck me."

Chapter Two

Renee

I hated that Monae hadn't talked to me about it but she was right. I was barely here and even if I was it wouldn't stop our bonding time that we had with each other because Brandon wasn't that type of guy.

Brandon had grown to be a respectful gentleman, to my sister anyway. They still did their dirt in the streets but he was her protector and he treated her like she was his queen.

In all of these years that he'd been around I had never seen them fight. As all of this went through my head I texted my sister that I was sorry and told her that I was happy for her and bro.

I was genuinely happy. Even more happy that I was on my way to my man house. Mario was older and wiser, especially in the bedroom. I loved spending time with him but tonight was going to be special.

My baby had gotten a promotion at work and tonight we would celebrate. He had planned for us to have a private dinner and movie then move to the hotel room for a private show in our room.

I couldn't wait. This was the first time that we had gotten a room and could be as free as we wanted to with each other. Yeah he lived alone but it was an apartment. Neighbors love hearing shit they shouldn't be listening to.

So as Mario and I chilled at his house I was on cloud nine from anticipation. We did some errand running just to get things done and kill some time. It was fun simply because I was with him. That's all that mattered.

Mario decided that today would be the day that I started driving. I had never driven before so I was a little terrified but he was right there to calm my nerves. He rubbed my back as I nervously grabbed the steering wheel.

"Just go slow. Don't worry about what anyone else says or does. Stay inside your lines and I'll guide you on the rest as we come to it." He said kissing my fear away

"Okay baby I trust you." I said as calm as I could

Next thing you know I was driving. It took me a few minutes to get a good feel for his car but after a few stop and go streets I was ready. He kept me on the side streets until I was ready for the main roads.

We never made it to the main road though because we weren't far from his apartment to begin with. Still I felt like I had gotten the hang of driving. But I planned on asking later for another lesson.

Once back to Mario's home we started packing for our date in a few hours. I had butterflies big time. I didn't know if it was due to my first time driving or the date but I needed to shake these butterflies.

I asked Mario "Baby would you by chance smoke with me?"

He looked at me strange and replied. "What type of question is that? For one, when did you start smoking? Two, why wouldn't I smoke with you? Three, where the hell did that come from?"

I couldn't help but laugh at his questioning and his facial expressions. He was genuinely caught off guard with my question. It was the cutest thing. I laughed for a while before answering him.

"I have smoked before. It's something that Monae

and I do to calm our nerves from time to time."

"Well let's get you relaxed baby." He said

We rolled up some amazing smelling goods and instantly I was on cloud nine. I didn't understand why I didn't come to him earlier. Shit me and sister could use this in our lives. But for real I was happy that he was helping me chill.

Once I got my nerves under control I was good to go. In fact his weed had me on go mode. I was horny as fuck and didn't want to wait until we got to the hotel. Mario insisted that we wait so that we could go at it full force.

I complied but I was twitching in my seat the entire time. I couldn't even drive again because I was so focused on riding his dick. Mario pulled out a blunt and handed it to me shaking his head.

"I hope this don't backfire on me but hit this and stop all of that fiending." He said laughing at me

I playfully snatched it from his grasp making sure that he saw me rolling my eyes. Then I sat back and sparked it up.

"It ain't my fault yo dick so damn good. Got me fiending like a junkie and shit."

He burst out laughing so hard I thought that we would crash. He kept it together though and we made it to the hotel in one peace. But we were high as fuck.

When we got to the room it was everything that I hoped for and more. The décor was beautiful and the bed was so soft. I held in the inner child in me that wanted to jump on the bed but it was hard.

Just then Mario left the room to go fill the ice bucket. It was the perfect timing for me to get in a few jumps. It was thrill seeking. Don't judge me though. I got out of the bed in time to make it up before he came back.

When he got back he put the wine on ice and set up the table with different fruits. Next he started to fill the jetted tub. He was being really romantic with his actions.

It was so nice to be pampered and treated like a queen. He undressed me then held my hand and led me to the tub where he helped me in. Next he did the same thing and joined me in the tub.

I couldn't help not keeping my hands to myself. Especially with this weed in my system I was on go mode. So I climbed on top of him in the jetted tub and began kissing him.

He welcomed me with open arms. It was such a great feeling. His kiss along with this water had me open and ready for what I was about to side down on. It felt so good. He was so big.

Once I got him all the way inside of me I rode my man like the world was about to end. Back and forth until I lost control and forced my tongue down his throat as I orgasmed hard.

It was not our first-time having sex but it was a different vibe. This night was one to remember for sure.

Chapter Three

Monae

Brandon had carried me downstairs and dropped me onto the bed. His strength turned me on and had me so fucking horny. I removed my dress revealing that I wasn't wearing anything underneath.

He bent down and began caressing my perky breast while he sucked on my erect nipples. I lost it when he did that. I started rubbing on his dick through his pants and he was ready.

As he grew older his dick grew bigger and better. That muthafucka was a monster waiting to kill my shit and I wanted it. I threw my legs in the air doing a little leg work for him while giving him a peek of my pussy.

He liked when I did that shit. I got wetter and he got harder. We were both always ready to go at it with each other because we knew that the other one was going to bring their A-game.

Brandon smirked at me so before he could take control I flipped over on my stomach and started twerking for him. He watched my ass bounce with such the biggest smile on his face.

I loved turning him on because he handled my little ass. Brandon smacked my ass and grabbed my head. I was already on the same thing as him so I opened my mouth and took him in.

My baby let out a soft moan and started feeding me the dick. Brandon wrapped my hair in his hand while he stroked my mouth feeding me the dick. With each stroke I tried to open my mouth more and more.

He was moaning like I'd never heard and that shit was getting me wetter by the moan. I wanted to feel him bust in my mouth just to feel like I had done my job but my pussy needed that dick.

I pulled back and licked my lips. He smiled and said "Got you with that tap out huh"?

"Not at all baby. I just want to feel that you stretch this pussy out." I said as I turned over

"Oohh damn baby. Well bend that ass over and let me see that pretty pussy."

I did as my baby said and bent over burying my face

into the bed while he got a good look at my dripping pussy. I could not wait to feel him enter me. Insertion was the best part of it all for me.

Once I felt him slide inside of me I couldn't hold it in. I moaned and came all over him immediately. He loved it. His strokes started off slow and teasing then they picked up. Harder not necessarily faster though.

Either way it was getting me wet as fuck. My moans got louder and louder with every stroke as he went deeper with his dick. I was on cloud nine as I began throwing it back at him.

We formed a rhythm and worked it out that way for a while before I just exploded all over his dick. Once I came he pulled out to admire my juices all over him.

I took advantage of this time to clean him off with my mouth. I licked down his shaft then back up until he slipped into my mouth. Together we tasted great which meant I tasted damn good.

But after I was full I spread my legs for my baby. He dove head first into his dinner and dessert. Brandon licked circles around my clitoris while he fingered my pussy and played with my ass.

He drove me insane with this shit. I came so hard and

when he drank me down I came even harder. It was the best oral sex ever. Hell I didn't need to be with someone else to know that my baby was skilled.

After convulsing from that orgasm he slammed his dick inside of me and pounded my shit. It felt so good that I was gushing the entire time. This was the first time that I had been this wet during sex.

Apparently Brandon was enjoying himself because when it was time for him to nut he didn't pull out. I felt him go harder and deeper until I felt that dick jerk. I knew then that he had came inside of me for the first time.

But I was too out of it and amazed by the sex to say anything or really care. It was all about feeling good and getting that nut so I was okay with it. Brandon pulled out and collapsed on the bed next to me.

We managed to get under the covers and fall asleep but that was about all that we did. When we awakened it was well after midnight. I had an appetite out of this world after all of that so I got up to fix us a snack.

Brandon slipped on his shorts and came upstairs with me. Even after all of that he came up the stairs looking sexy as fuck to me and I couldn't help but get wet all over again.

I bit my lip and watched him stretch showing off all of his muscles. I rushed that man and jumped into his arms for another round right there in the kitchen. He didn't stop me either. My babe was ready.

He tossed me up in the air and when I came down he had pulled his dick out that quick and was sliding it in me. The look on his face as he stared into my eyes gave me chills. It was so real, so deep, just serious and sexy.

We went at it until he came again because sex ain't shit if my man don't get his. Fuck pleasing me because I'm going to cum as soon as he enters me but I want to see him blow.

When Brandon let me down he kissed me in a way that I had never experienced before. Something had changed with him. GiGi had said new things would occur but I didn't think it would happen so quick.

More importantly is that I didn't really know if this change was for the better or worse. I guess only time would tell. For now I was going to enjoy the ride. Literally, enjoy the ride.

Chapter Four

Renee

We had a blast at the hotel but it was now time to check out and get back to reality. I didn't want to leave my baby side but he had to work and I had to go home and check on big sis.

Although I knew that she could take care of herself we vowed as children to always be there for one another and I took that serious. I knew that she had Brandon to watch after her but that was my sister.

On the way home Mario put me to the challenge again and had me drive us to my house. It was a further distance so I got more practice in. He was so supportive and it was great to have his support. It made me feel comfortable.

I did really well and was proud of my accomplishment. Sadly, when I got home I couldn't even share my excitement with my sister because she wasn't there. I called her and it went to voicemail.

I thought nothing of it and carried on with the day. I went to see GiGi but she wasn't home either. She hadn't been staying home much now that we were legally old enough to fend for ourselves.

Can't say that I blame her though. She was done raising kids then here comes her grandchildren to stay. We cut into her life and she adjusted like a champ. For that I would always respect, love, and cherish her.

I took advantage of my free time and cleaned the house. It wasn't dirty because we didn't get down like that but some extra tlc couldn't hurt. I went into the kitchen to start there and as soon as I did I heard glass crashing.

I ran into the living room and found a big ass brick in the middle of the room. Somebody had thrown a big ass brick threw our living room window. Before I could even reach the door I saw a car speeding away.

There was no way that I saw what I saw. It was David's car but he was dead so who was harassing me now. I was terrified now knowing that someone was trying to get back at me for David. Even in death this nigga was a pain in my ass.

Whoever it was knew where I lived so what else did they know about me. I called up Monae and again it rang until it reached voicemail. Where the fuck was she? I was beyond panicking at this point.

Next, I called up Brandon. It wasn't unusual for me to reach out to him every once in a while but he always knew that it was somewhat important to me if I reached out myself.

"Yo what's up sis?" He answered

"Bruh somebody just threw a damn brick threw our living room window! And that's not all. Whoever did it was driving David's car." I replied

"What the fuck!? How the hell is this shit happening? I'm coming back to the house sis. Be cool." He told me

I was a nervous wreck, but I was playing it cool for everyone else. But how could I relax when someone out there wanted to hurt me and I had no clue who it was. This wasn't good.

I sat rocking back and forth until Brandon got here. It didn't take him long because he was a dope boy after all so he was always on the move. Bruh got here and was pissed when he saw the damage.

He was tightening his jaw and breathing heavy. I could tell that he was going to do damage to whoever was responsible for this shit. Bruh didn't play when it came to his girlfriends safety.

And considering that she lived here too I'm sure that he was hot about this shit. Thinking about his girlfriend made me ask him where she was.

"Hey Brandon, where is Monae? I've been calling her and she won't answer."

"She's at work. That's where I was when you called." He replied without looking at me

He was breaking the rest of the glass that was left in the window. I got the broom to begin sweeping but he was agitated and took the broom from me to do it himself.

I didn't know why he was so pissed but he was turning red and didn't want to be bothered. Not even from me helping him. So I went and sat outside for some fresh air and to relax.

Life was good but it seemed that it was getting the best of me. Monae had a steady man in her life and was working now. Meanwhile I had no job and I was falling for Mario but what else did I have besides a new stalker.

I began crying on the porch and that was a horrible thing to do. As soon as I started here came the nosey muthafuckas from the neighborhood. Everyone wanted to know what was wrong but no one was really going to help.

So I just told everyone that I missed my dad which wasn't a complete lie, I did miss him. Right before I got up to go in one more person approached me. It was a neighbor of ours who had moved in a few years ago but remained quiet and kept to himself.

"Hey it's Renee, right?"

"Yeah" I said as I cleaned my face yet again

"I don't mean to pry but are you sure that you're okay?" He said so sincere

"No but I will be, thanks. Sorry I don't remember your name." I told him

"It's Ashton. Is there anything that I can do for you? You want to come by for a drink?" He offered

"I don't drink but maybe I can come by just to get acquainted."

He smiled and agreed. Of course, this wasn't a smart idea but I just wanted to get out of Brandon's hair. So I went a few doors down to Ashton's house and we talked for a while.

Hours had passed and I felt like I had told him my entire life story. He didn't seem to care how much I talked and the crazy thing is that he was attentive the entire time.

I stood up to go and was met toe to toe with his tall slim frame. His scent stopped me in my tracks. Next thing I knew I had my tongue down this man's throat. His hands caressed my body sending chills down my spine.

He pushed me down on the couch and stood over me removing his belt. I knew what I was about to do was wrong but I couldn't help myself.

Chapter Five

Monae

My first day at work was a good one simply because I was excited to have a job. It was a clerical job so I sat in a cubicle most of the day but the atmosphere was happy at all times.

It was a small office space but they provided us with snacks, drinks, and exercise equipment to keep us motivated throughout the day. I was happy to be a productive citizen and bring my own money home.

Don't get me wrong I never needed for anything thanks to GiGi and Brandon but I wanted more for myself. I wanted more for my sister too. She needed something to do because she was blowing me up today.

When I took break I finally called her back but I got no answer. It was normal for her to ignore me especially if she was with her boo thang but not after she was frantically calling me.

I called Brandon and asked if he had seen her and he explained what happened at home. That pissed me off but what could I do about it right now. That was my only downfall about working.

I was trapped here on their watch for eight hours of my day. I was used to being free to pop up when and where I wanted to.

After calming down and getting back to work it seemed like the day flew by because I was so focused on what to do when I got home. Thankfully, I didn't have to wait on a window crew because my baby took care of that.

He told me that Renee left crying and that he hadn't seen her since then. That made me furious because I knew my sister and that meant she was up to no good.

I sent her a text that said to get home and stay there until we figured out who wanted to hurt her ass but I never got a reply back. When I got off work you better believe that I was ready to go to war with her and everyone else in my path.

"How was your day gorgeous?" Asked Brandon

"It was good until this bullshit happened." I spat back

"Don't let that ruin your day baby. I took care of the window. Even did it before GiGi got home and saw anything." He said as he raised my hand and kissed it

He made me feel at ease. I was comfortable with him around but his new found love that he was pouring into me was something different. I liked it but I didn't know if it were permanent.

"Thank you for taking care of the house today. I can't wait to find Renee's ass and beat her ass." I said as we pulled up to the house

I walked into the house expecting my sister to be there but of course she wasn't. It was hours later before she strolled her ass into the house singing. I let her get close then I punched her ass in the face.

"Bitch stop doing that shit! Why the fuck did you hit me in the fucking face?" She yelled holding her nose

"Why the fuck are you out kicking it and someone wants your ass hurt or dead? Why blow me up then don't answer my calls? Where were you?" I yelled back

"Minding my business, why?" She snapped back

"Bitch you don't have business. All of your business requires you spreading your funky ass legs." I said throwing another blow to her head

She grabbed me by my hair and tried to fling me to the ground but I swung my body causing her to hit the wall. She yelled because she hit her back on the corner of the wall.

I used that brief distraction and moment of pain to throw a punch to her side which made her drop to the ground. But my sister was no quitter. She twisted around to her back and kicked me.

Her kick sent me flying backwards as I stumbled. That angered me. I ran back to her and kicked her twice not really caring where my kick landed. This was by far the worst fight that we ever had in our lives.

In my mind she deserved every blow that landed on her ass because she was already being reckless with her life. That's when I felt Brandon pull me off of her.

"Baby stop it. You gone kill her!"

"Good, better me than whoever busted our damn window." I said still trying to throw blows

Renee was on the floor crying and bleeding. I looked down at her and told her to get out of my face. But I knew that was impossible because we lived together and even I didn't want GiGi to know about this fight.

Brandon pulled me away from Renee but I was still swinging. He had to throw me down to get me to stop swinging and calm down. Eventually I did then I started crying but I didn't let Renee see it.

I never wanted to hurt my sister but sometimes she would be really careless and I hated that. And for that she needed to be taught a lesson. I crawled into bed and cried myself to sleep.

Brandon returned to Renee to help her get cleaned up. I couldn't be mad at him for helping her. It actually made me realize that he cared about us more than I realized.

That night Renee didn't come back to her room. This was the first night that anyone had stayed in dad's room but that's where she slept. I'm glad too because I didn't want to see her hurting like that especially knowing that I was the cause.

Life was pulling me in so many directions and my emotions were all over the place. I had to get a grip on things. As I lay there thinking about how I hurt my sister I could hear Brandon's words in my head.

"Baby stop it! You gone kill her." Those words hurt my heart because I knew what I was capable of and his words very well could have come true but he didn't know that.

I sat up in bed and thought to myself. If Brandon was really down for me and we were planning the murder of his former best friend together then it was time for me to come clean about my past.

I just hope this didn't backfire on me.

Chapter Six

Renee

Ashton had given me some much-needed stress relief but it meant nothing when I returned home. Monae had gotten home from work and she was on one big time. As soon as I got there she hit me like I was a fucking nobody.

I was tired of her putting her hands on me so this time I swung back at her. Things only escalated from there. We had the worst fight that we had ever had with each other in our entire lives.

And if that was not enough, she left me bloody and hurting on the living room floor screaming get out of her face the entire time. She had turned into the damn devil and I was praying hard for God to help me win this battle.

It did not happen that way though. She beat my ass then left me to die because that was how I was feeling, like I was facing death. I couldn't move at all. My breathing was at a minimal. Right now I just wanted to be with my dad.

I felt someone pick me up and I thought for a second that somehow an ambulance had been called for me. But it was only my imagination. The hands that I felt were those of Brandon.

He had felt sorry for me and came to assist in getting me cleaned up and in bed. I cried the entire time not wanting to go downstairs with the monster that tried to kill me so he helped me into dad's room.

"How could she do me that way? Her twin Brandon! This ain't right." I cried

"I know sis. She took things too far. I'll talk to her but I don't promise any results. Just get some rest and I'll take you to the hospital tomorrow after she goes to work. Cool?" He said

"Thank you" I whispered as I prepared to cry myself to sleep.

I didn't know who that girl was that hurt me in such a way then walked away from me without talking. Monae always talked to me about whatever she felt I had done wrong. She never bit her tongue with me.

Eventually I cried myself to sleep and the pain went away. But I was hurting so bad when I awakened that I couldn't move. It took all of my might and twenty minutes to get up for the bathroom.

I could hear my phone going off while I was in the bathroom. Mario was calling me but I couldn't answer. There was no way that I could tell him what Monae had done. They already had a rocky start so this would only send them back to that point.

This was something that I had to deal with on my own. I managed to get undressed and into the bathtub. Once I was in the tub I ran the water and let it soothe some of my aches and pains.

I sat in there for as long as I could before the water started to cool down. Then I washed myself as best as I could. I got out and stood there staring at myself in the mirror.

My body was bruised but not as bad as I thought it would be. Shit I felt like I was dying last night and I was sore as hell today but I managed. I got dressed slowly to avoid causing unnecessary pains.

Once I managed to do all of that on my own I sat and cried hard. This was the worst time of my life. I had someone out there wanting to do harm to me and my sister had turned her back on me after beating my ass.

I wanted to call Mario so bad and cry to him but I couldn't. That wouldn't end well for Monae and only I could be responsible for the hurting she deserved. My trust had been broken by her actions and only time would tell if it could be healed.

Just as my melt down was coming to an end I heard the front door slam closed. Being too sore to spring to my feet fear took over and I sat there ready for what or whoever was coming for me.

"Sis, what's up? What's going on? You in here crying hella loud. I heard you outside." Said Brandon

"Sorry bro. I just hate being helpless and I'm still pissed that Monae did this to me."

"Yeah she was out of line. I talked to her on the ride to work but of course she wasn't trying to hear any of what I was saying." Brandon said sounding extremely sad

I started crying harder. In a matter of years my life had been changed in so many ways. None of the ways were good either. I had nothing going for myself but trouble. How did I end up this way?

"Renee? Are you hearing me?"

"No, sorry. What did you say?" I asked

"Do you want to go to the hospital? You know they're going to ask who did it."

"I wouldn't tell but no I don't want to go. I just want to get far away from here." I replied

"I'm sorry sis." He said as he backed away

I didn't know what was going on with him but he was showing a softer side and Monae hadn't noticed yet because she was busy being a bitch to everybody. I was beginning to hate calling this place home.

Brandon went into the kitchen and I could hear him rummaging around in the cupboards. I reached for my phone and phoned a friend. He answered and agreed to come help me escape this hell hole.

I got up and managed to make it to the door. When I opened it I saw him standing there waiting on me. Ashton looked shocked but rushed to my side to help me out of the house.

He asked me if I could walk the distance and I guess I looked scared because the next thing I knew he had swept me off my feet. Ashton had picked me up and carried me to his house and it was over after that.

Chapter Seven

Monae

I had made it through the work day without any errors or problems so my day was okay for the most part. What was about to change that was the going home part. I was really in no mood to deal with my dumb ass sister.

Brandon was here to pick me up promptly like always. He had been acting a little different and I wanted to call him on it but I chose not to. I wanted to sit back and watch then react.

"So how was your day babe?"

"It was actually pretty good. How were things at home?"

"Well Renee is pretty fucked up but not too bad because I went to fix breakfast but she left while I was in the kitchen cooking." He said with a shrug

"First of all fuck you for trying to help the ungrateful.

Secondly, good. I'm glad she was able to get the fuck out."

I noticed him cringe at what I had said but I didn't care. He could go too if he felt so strongly about a sibling rivalry. On the way home I told Brandon to stop and get us dinner because I didn't feel like cooking.

He gave me a nasty look that I didn't like. Then he said "I can cook dinner again if you want."

"What do you mean again?" I inquired

"Well for the past week or so you have been mean and unmoved to do anything besides go to work."

"Did you just call me lazy?"

"No but if the shoe fits wear it." He said with an attitude

"What is your problem?! You've been on some bull-shit lately. Get over it." I yelled at him

He didn't say anything. We rode in silence to get dinner then he made a stop at the drug store. I didn't ask him what for nor did I get out with him. I guess he didn't care because he never looked back when he got out.

I waited for all of five minutes for him to come back.

When he did he threw the bag at me. I caught it to throw back but I saw what was in it. This negro had gone in the store and bought a pregnancy test.

Again the car ride was silent but this time from my shock at his purchase. How did he figure that I could be pregnant? What did that have to do with anything? I was now filled with fear and sadness.

What if I was pregnant? How would my life change? I wasn't ready to be a mom. As all of these questions went through my mind I began to think and get angry.

"You did this shit on purpose!" I yelled as I threw the test back at him and got out of the car.

"What the fuck are you talking about?" He said trying to play it cool

"Don't play dumb with me. You've been nutting in me for a while now. You were trying to get me pregnant."

"Yeah and I figured you were fine with it since you never had an objection to it. So watch your fucking tone. You ain't innocent." He said glaring at me

"Just because I didn't object doesn't mean that I would keep it." I shot back

"I wish you would. You might as well kill yourself if you do that Monae."

"Was that a threat Brandon?" I asked walking up to him

We were standing face to face with neither of us backing down. He looked down on me and responded.

"Try me." Then he backed away slowly.

I had never feared him before but right now I had mixed emotions. Something in me told me that he was dead ass serious. What parent wouldn't kill over there child, even one unborn.

I picked up the bag that held the pregnancy test and headed to my room. Brandon had walked outside so I ran with the bag downstairs. I prayed over the test that it would be negative then I proceeded to open it.

The minutes went by so slow as I waited. Finally I looked at the clock and time was up. I closed my eyes as I inched forward towards the stick. When I opened my eyes I noticed Brandon had snuck downstairs and was standing behind me.

"So what does it say?" He questioned

I looked down at the test and tears instantly filled

my eyes. "It says that we are not pregnant!" There I stood crying happy tears while Brandon gave me the stare of death. I didn't care, I did not want kids.

Now that I knew what he was on I would have to play things a little differently. I waited for him to exit the bathroom then I pulled out my phone. It was time for me to make an appointment for birth control.

I would have GiGi take me to keep it from Brandon. That way he could keep doing what he was doing and thinking that he would one day get a child. I mean one day he would but it probably wouldn't be with me.

Don't get me wrong I loved that man but he was a damn fool if he thought that I was going to give up my freedom to sit home with a kid. That wasn't a part of the plan.

I threw the test in the garbage can and washed my hands with a smile on my face. Things were about to change around here and I couldn't wait. It was time for Monae Centric to shine.

Chapter Eight

Renee

I had managed to get away from that house. The one that held so many memories and used to bring me happiness. It was now a place of horror and torture.

Monae had destroyed all the happy memories in a matter of minutes. She was no longer my responsibility. Besides she was the oldest anyway so why should I look out for her. She proved she was capable of taking care of herself.

Ashton had carried me to his house and helped wrap the wounds that needed to be protected. He rubbed an ointment on me that burned at first causing me to scream out in pain at first.

But as it started to work the burning cooled down and I felt relief. It actually made me feel like I could get up and move. My pain had subsided. I don't know what he had put on me but I was thankful.

"Have you eaten breakfast yet?"

"No, I left as soon as I could. Being in the house made me hurt even more. I thought I was going to die but whatever you just put on me feels great."

"It's just a little mixture that I whipped up. Glad it's working for you."

He had walked into his kitchen and I could hear him opening cabinets and ripping packages open. After about ten minutes he returned with a bowl of soup and some hot tea.

I was expecting more but he knew what he was doing. Ashton told me that the soup was good for my healing process. He said that my body wouldn't have fight to heal while toxins destroyed things on the inside.

This man sounded crazy to me but he assured me that if I were in the hospital I would only be eating soups and drinking clear liquids. He won the argument with that statement.

I ate the soup and drank the tea. While I was sitting there explaining what had happened Ashton began giving me a massage. He was so gentle. His hands were like magic. I fell asleep in his arms.

When I awakened I could hear him in the other room playing his game. I slowly got up and walked toward the sound of his voice. He had company which startled me when I peeked around the door.

"What's up Renee? Did I wake you?" Asked Ashton

"No, you're good. I was just getting up and heading to the bathroom. Sorry to interrupt." I said turning to walk down the hall to the bathroom

He walked behind me in silence. I only knew he was there because of his scent. He always smelled so good. It was definitely a turn on for me. Once I reached the bathroom door I turned to face him.

"Is there something you need?" I asked softly

He gently put his hands on my waist and pulled me in close to him. He stared into my eyes and replied. "You" Then he leaned down and began kissing me.

The kiss was like something out of a fairy tale story. So sweet and gentle yet demanding. His tongue found its way inside of my mouth and introduced itself to mine. It wasn't the first time we kissed but it was the first time that any feeling was behind it.

I felt my knees get weak and almost buckle. This man was doing something to me. He wasn't supposed to have this effect on me. Lord I was in for trouble when I finally talked to Mario.

Although I missed him I still hadn't called him. I know he had to be worried sick. I made a mental note to text him when I got back to my phone. Meanwhile I stood there in Ashton's grasp feeling loved.

He released me and I stood frozen until my bladder reminded me to get moving. I used the bathroom but kept wondering why he was being so nice to me and what I was doing here.

I made my way back to the living room then started cleaning my mess. His friend exited the room and walked outside. Ashton soon followed. I was confused as to whether or not he was leaving so I tried to see out of the window.

That was a bad idea because I fell trying to move quickly. It wasn't a bad fall but it did hurt like hell. I was aching all over again. Ashton came back in the house and caught me rubbing my side.

"What happened? You in pain?"

"Yeah, I took a tumble and now I'm a bit sore again."

"You just can't sit still and let me take care of you huh?"

"I can take care of myself."

"Sure, so you called me and I carried you over to my house so that you can take care of yourself?"

I rolled my eyes at him but he had a point. I couldn't do this shit on my own. He was helping more than I ever could have done for myself. My dependence on Monae was starting to be evident.

"So, do you want my help or should I help you go back home?" He said standing at the door

I broke down crying like a baby. Ashton secured the door and took a seat next to me.

"Look do you want my help or not?" He asked

"Yes"

"Okay so understand that I'm not the bad guy here. You have to work with me not against me."

I nodded then he wiped my tears away. I don't know why but when this man touched me it sent tingles down my spine and I got goosebumps every time. Something about him was mysterious yet comforting.

For now I would have to trust in him but soon I would no longer be fragile little Renee. I was about to fly solo and take care of my little problem before it was too late.

Chapter Nine

Monae

It had been days since I had seen Renee or even talked to her. I guess my twin senses knew that she was fine but I decided to check on her anyway. I called her up but she didn't answer so I texted her.

She replied a few minutes later saying that she was okay but I wanted to know where she was. Renee told me that she was out with a friend and that she was fine so I left it alone.

I sat at home enjoying the quietness on my day off. It felt good to sit home with no one here to piss me off. Just as I was about to run my bath there was a knock at the door.

It was Mario. Not who I cared to see but I figured Renee had sent him for some of her clothes. I opened the door and walked away. I was heading back to my bathroom when he stopped me.

"Aye, did I do something to everyone?"

"What are you talking about?"

"Well Renee won't answer her phone for me. She just text me from time to time so I showed up here and you just walked away from me without a hello."

I had a look of confusion on my face. I could tell because his face started to reflect mine.

"What happened? Where is she?" He demanded

"I don't know where she is. I thought she had been with you all this time and that you were coming to get some clothes for her. That's why I opened the door and walked away."

He sat down on the couch and pulled out his phone. I watched as he dialed Renee's number. No answer. He showed me that she had sent him to voicemail.

I picked up my phone and dialed her too. Same thing. Now I was concerned. A minute later Mario's phone rang back with a text message from Renee. He demanded to talk to her but she gave an excuse why she couldn't.

This was unlike her at all. I understood being angry with me still but not with Mario. She loved him too damn much to not talk to him or see him in days. What was going on?

I thought that maybe she would text me back something more but she didn't even text me at all. I won't even lie my feelings were hurt. She was my sister after all and I wanted to know that she was okay.

"Mario keep trying to get her to talk to you and try asking around for her. I honestly don't know where she would be if she isn't with you." I said

"Okay but why would she do this? What made her leave home without saying a word?"

Just then Brandon walked through the door. He looked at me then at Mario before speaking.

"What's going on?" Asked Brandon

"No one knows where Renee is and she won't answer her phone for anyone." I replied

He gave me a weird look and a tilt of the head. Now Mario was looking at me strange. I just needed her to bring her ass home and clear this shit up. She needed to grow the hell up.

"You gone tell him or shall I?" Said Brandon

"Tell me what? Somebody better start fucking talking!" Snapped Mario

Before I could speak Brandon started singing like a fucking canary.

"Monae and Renee had a fight. An actual fist fight and Monae beat her up pretty bad. Wherever she is she's bruised up and hurting."

I could see the fire in Mario's eyes and I'm sure he would have lounged at me if it wasn't for Brandon standing there. Not that I cared though. He could have tried his luck.

"Look what happened between me and my sister is a sibling thing but we need to find her. Or did we all forget that she has someone out there trying to harm her?" I said

"Oh I'm very aware of it but you do realize that this is your fault right?" Said Mario

"My fault? I'm not responsible for her actions."

"Bullshit! Find her and bring her ass home." Mario said walking towards me with his hands in fists

"Get the fuck out of my house and don't ever step foot back in here. I don't care if she comes back in two minutes, you're not welcome here." I yelled at him

"Bitch if I catch you alone it's over for you." He said as he stormed out of the door

Now I had a situation to deal with myself. All because this girl wanted to run away like we're fucking kids. I swear I would beat her ass again once she healed.

"You still don't see what you've done do you?" Asked Brandon breaking me from my trance

"You can get the fuck out too because I didn't do a damn thing." I said to him

Without saying anything more he grabbed his keys and his hat then headed out of the door. I hated to see him go because he looked so good when he did but he had me fucked up talking to me like that.

I texted Renee that she needed to get home ASAP but I got no response. I swear when I find her she was going to need Jesus on her side and as if things weren't already bad enough in walked GiGi. "Sit down Monae. We need to talk."

Chapter Ten

Renee

Something was going on because my phone was blowing up. I didn't answer any of the calls but I made sure to respond to Mario via text. Other than that I didn't care.

Brandon had reached out to me too and ignoring his call actually made me feel bad. He had tried to help me and he was on my side. I just couldn't chance Monae being with him if I answered.

Me and Ashton had been sitting on the couch with me straddling him when there was knock at the door. We both looked at each other strange and with disappointment on our faces.

He lifted me to the side and stood there adjusting himself before answering the door. I was wearing a smile because I knew what he was trying to hide was not easily concealable.

Ashton stood at the door for a minute before instructing me to go into the bedroom. I was now nervous. Who was on the other side of the door still knocking?

When he opened the door I was listening hard trying to figure out if I recognized the voice. I heard a familiar voice and wanted to run out there but I had to keep my location private.

"What's up?" Said Ashton

"Hey, I know Renee is here. Can I talk to her?" Said Brandon

"Nah she ain't here but if I run into her I'll let her know that you were looking for her. Who are you again?" Questioned Ashton

"I'm her brother. And y'all don't have to worry I didn't tell Monae where she is and I don't plan to."

Just like that I heard him start to walk down the stairs. I wanted to talk to Brandon. I started to cry as I ran out to the living room window. I watched him get in his car solo and leave.

I used this time to call him. It was the only phone call that I had made in over a week. He answered immediately.

"Renee?"

"Yeah it's me. What's going on?"

"Things are pretty bad at home. Mario came by looking for you and asking questions. I told him what happened that made you leave and that caused an argument. He told Monae to find you before he kills her." I heard him say

"Why should I care? She tried to kill me. I'm still healing from the ass whooping she gave me. I don't care about her and I'm not coming home." I said as tears started to fall

"Well you know that doesn't leave any other option, right?" He said

"Well brother I guess we all gotta do what we gotta do."

I hated to hang up on him in such a fashion but I had to get off of the phone with him before my conscience kicked in. He was the only person that I felt had my back right now but he loved my evil sister.

I gathered my thoughts and cleaned my tears before facing Ashton again. He moved closer to me on the couch and began to wipe my face for me. I was beginning to think that I was a weak bitch with all of these tears.

"So what's your problem with your sister? As I stated a minute ago I'm here for you."

"I appreciate that and I don't know what to do. I have bigger issues than my stupid ass sister."

"Okay, you gone tell me what all I need to know? I mean I am the one housing you and you seem to have a lot of bullshit following you."

I was offended by his statement but it was true. My problems would follow me no matter where I went. I needed to deal with them asap. Now I had to figure out where to spend my days while I mapped things out.

"Can I stay here for a few while I figure things out? I don't know exactly how long but I promise not to get in your way." I asked him

"Renee you don't ever have to leave if you don't want to. I introduced myself for a reason. I knew that you needed a friend and I'm willing to be that plus more." He said as he caressed my cheek

I leaned into his chest as his hand guided my face to his. Our kiss was anything less than amazing. This man took my breath away with the most innocent touch.

He led the kiss and I followed by climbing into his lap. We were back to what we were getting into before Brandon came knocking. I was ready. With all of this excitement going on I needed a fix.

Ashton took his time with me unlike anyone else. I mean he was even more gentle and attentive than Mario. I let him have his way with me with no regrets.

The way that he caressed my body and eased inside of me had me on fire already. Then the ride was mine to control. I rode him while looking into his eyes and running my fingers through his hair.

It felt so right. I kept coming and he kept slowly thrusting to match my rodeo motion. I closed my eyes and got lost in feeling. His soft moans kept going more.

Then his hands traveled up my back and held me down as he took control. His thrust became stronger and harder. Our bodies were one as he thrust one last time and came so hard.

I had no care in the world as I looked into his eyes and kissed him. His soul spoke to me in that moment and I collapsed in his arms. It wasn't until minutes later that I realized my mistake.

I had foolishly made love to this man without a condom and he had cum inside of me. The fear that crept through my mind was short lived when he grabbed my face and kissed me.

Ashton made all of my worries go away without even trying. All he had to say was "Don't worry I got you."

Chapter Eleven

Monae

I had been fuming ever since that punk ass boyfriend of Renee had come by here. He had his nerve! And then to demand that I find her or else was something I took serious.

He had no right to threaten me. And punk ass Brandon allowed the bullshit. But my absolute favorite part of that night was GiGi coming to have a talk. That was anything but good.

She had instructed me to sit down and chat with her. I was not in the mood but I couldn't really say no to her. The look she was giving me made my stomach turn.

"Now I tried to mind my own business and let you do you but I see that didn't work."

"GiGi I ain't no babysitter. I didn't sign up for this."

"And I didn't sign up to lose my daughter so tragic either. I didn't sign up to gain two more children to raise.

I didn't sign up to take yo shit. You get my drift?"

I rolled my eyes but answered her. "Yeah I get it."

"Now what the fuck is going on over here and damn it Monae don't you lie to me."

I told her everything that had happened. Of course, she was more concerned with where Renee was than the fact that a psycho wanted to harm me. It was really starting to piss me off that everyone always cared about the whore more.

"GiGi it's not fair that no one seems to care about my well-being but they always cry for her stupidity. She needs to learn to deal with her problems herself."

"And if she can't? What if she fails and is killed out here trying to be somebody she's not?"

I looked at her strange. What the fuck did that mean?

"She's not as street smart as you Monae. You have always taken care of her because that's your sister but you also know that she is not as hard ass compared to you too." GiGi explained

I sighed because she was right. Renee was good with her body, not thinking. I still didn't feel like I needed to bring her home or fight her battles for her. She needed to do that on her own.

GiGi continued to 'school me' except this time I wasn't listening. I was thinking of how I was going to lure Renee out of hiding so I could feed her to the wolves.

She had to go. I had my own life to live and I was seeing now that meant dropping a lot of people from my circle because they didn't understand me. I wanted to live free.

Yeah, I thought about just moving to another state but why should I run? Besides that wasn't my style. After tuning GiGi out for a while I figured I would acknowledge her.

"Okay GiGi. I'll find her. I'll right my wrong with my twin. We all we got, right?"

She looked at me and nodded. If I knew my grandmother she was probably cursing me out in her head and calling me all kind of unholy names. But she would never say them out loud because it wasn't her character.

GiGi took her time leaving and I didn't rush her. I simply went downstairs to my room to put my plan into motion. I had to find this scaredy cat. I called her phone and left her a voicemail this time.

"Renee I'm really sorry about the fight and hurting you. I need you to come back home so that we can be one again. I need you so that we can fight together not with each other. Please come home." I said hoping that I sounded like I was crying

Next, I tried to see if there was any way of tracking a cell phone. There were plenty of websites out there saying that you could but of course you needed the phone to be present in order to install software.

I researched so much information on how to find someone yet I was still clueless on how to track her ass down. And it was hard to begin to search for her when she could wiggle her ass and get any man to help her.

But something told me to start close to home. As I headed outside to go for a walk just to clear my mind I saw a tone of people out. I decided to try my hand at some face to face conversation/interrogation.

First up was a group of children playing double dutch and football nearby. I walked up to them and asked if they had seen my sister. They said not in a while then one of the little bastards asked if she was dead.

I don't know why that bothered me as much as it did

but I had to correct the child.

"Aye look here don't wish ill on my sister! Watch your mouth and if you see her come find me immediately." I said as I gave them all a few dollars

Further down the street was some older guys from the neighborhood. I approached them and they all spoke to me. It was no secret of who I was thanks to GiGi and Brandon.

"What's up Monae?" Said a familiar face

I turned to see who it was and it was the geeky kid that lived up the street from us in the other direction. I acknowledged him but didn't pay him no mind. I had a job to do.

He looked at me weird because I spoke and kept it moving. Shit I didn't know him. Hell I didn't even recall his name. Then he spoke again. This time about my sister.

"You looking for your sister?"

"Yeah what you know about it?" I questioned him

"I mean I seen her a few days ago at the mall with another blonde hair chick and an average dark skinned nigga. She spoke to me and kept it pushing." He said shrugging his shoulders

I thought about who the female was that he could have been describing but drew a blank. Just then the description of the guy came to me. It was Mario bitch ass. I didn't have solid proof but I'm sure it was. Where else could she be?

Chapter Twelve

Renee

Things had been super chaotic ever since Mario popped up at the house looking for me. I wanted to end all of this madness but I was in no mood to go back to that house.

I had been relaxing as best as I could with Ashton. Although I barely knew him he was taking care of me and making me feel comfortable. I was in no rush to leave. This was much needed healing.

The only draw back to this arrangement was me missing Mario. I decided to call him up one day when Ashton went out. I would soon find out that was a bad move. To say I regretted making the call was an understatement.

Instead of being happy to hear from me, Mario flipped the fuck out. I had never heard him yell at me in such a way. It made me feel like all of our times together were fake and that this was truly how he felt.

"Mario why are you being so mean about a situation that has nothing to do with you?"

"Because Renee you don't know how to stand up for yourself. You always bow down to your sister and that shit needs to stop. I need a woman by my side not a baby."

"Wow. That hurt Mario."

"Well do something about it."

"Oh I will. Trust me. There will be a lot of changes coming."

"What does that mean?" He inquired

"Just means that I will be standing up for myself real soon."

And with that I ended the call. Who would have thought that he would be so cold towards me. My mind was racing because without talking to Monae I wouldn't know who the real enemy was.

I thought about things and came to the conclusion that I would talk to my sister once and for all. I texted her to meet me at the park tomorrow around noon.

She agreed to do it only if it happened today so I said

never mind. This was going to be done on my time not hers. I was tired of her running the show. This was my time to shine and get shit done.

Eventually Monae texted me back because I hadn't said anything after that and I wasn't begging her ass for a meeting. She agreed to meet me tomorrow at noon and I was excited. Now I could carry out the rest of my plans for the day.

I was healed physically and now it was time for me to heal mentally. Ashton called me interrupting my thoughts.

"Hello"

"Hey Renee, your sister is out looking for you. She's straight paying people for information about you. I told her that I saw you at the mall last week with a blonde and an average dude."

"That's low as fuck for her to be paying people. She's up to something. Did you find out anything or why she's looking for me?"

"Nah, she didn't really want to talk to me. She turned her nose up to me so I'm sure she doesn't suspect that you're across the street in my house."

"Well that's a damn good thing. I'll see you when you

get home. And by the way I cooked."

I can tell that he was smiling as he said okay before hanging up. This man was giving me reason to this fucked up life. He never sweated the small stuff and he never rushed anywhere.

Everything that Ashton did was on his time and his level. I admired that so much. I was learning his ways. That's why I wouldn't allow Monae to rush me into meeting with her.

Ashton owned everything that he did or touched all the way down to his geeky look. I had gotten to see a different side of him. A man without his glasses, without his clothes, without a care, and without his guard up.

His confidence was amazing. And the fact that he had taken me under his wing without a second thought said that he was a caring man. I was thankful to him for all that he had done thus far so cooking dinner for him was nothing.

Ashton came right home after I said that I cooked. He immediately went to get clean before coming to the table. You could tell that this man was raised right. He showed mad respect for women and just life in general.

"So what did you cook?" He said walking into the kitchen

"Just a little baked chicken, macaroni, cornbread, and green beans. With a cake in the oven." I said with a smile

"Damn, you really laid it down huh?"

"Not yet" I said as I winked at him and rubbed his chest

"Damn..." Was all he could say as he bent down and kissed me

I made him a plate and sat it on the table before making my own. I had waited for him to get home to eat so that we could bond a little. We hadn't sat down to get to know each other and I wanted to know more about him.

Plus I wanted to tell him about my plan to meet with Monae tomorrow. I didn't want to go alone in case she came playing dirty. I waited until he was almost finished before bringing it up though.

"Hey, so I reached out to Monae and she agreed to meet with me tomorrow to talk."

"Where? Cuz I'm not letting you go alone. She's a

shady ass bitch that tried to take you out once so what makes you think she won't try it again. I'm going." He said sternly

"Okay but I'm capable of handling business by myself." I said folding my arms

"I know you are but I'll be damned if she try anything on you again because I'm not having it. That's my word." He said pushing his plate back and leaning forward

"So what's your plan?" He asked

I couldn't even hide the smile that was plastered on my face right now. He had made me happy with standing on coming with me to protect me. That meant that he cared about me plus I wanted him there too.

We spent the next couple of hours cleaning the kitchen and talking over what to say to her and how to get the most out of the meeting. I needed to know everything that she was thinking.

Plus I still had a psycho out there after me and I hadn't been home so who knows what or if anything had happened since the last incident. I had so much on my mind but I had a goal and I was determined to stick with it.

Chapter Thirteen

Monae

Renee had reached out to me wanting to meet up and talk. I was ready to get to her too. She needed to bring her ass home so that we could get to the bottom of a few things.

One of those things was shutting up her punk ass boyfriend Mario. I bet he was hiding her out at his place and just pretending that she was missing to help her crybaby ass.

When I find out that's what is happening I'll beat her ass again only worse this time. And that muthafucka had it coming too. Nobody yelled at me and threatened me like that, especially in my own home.

I would keep my cool until then but I had a feeling that's where she was. The guy across the street confirmed it when he said that he had seen Renee at the mall with a guy and a girl.

Who else could it have been? She didn't have many friends outside of me and Brandon. I was becoming more annoyed by the minute waiting on tomorrow to come so that I could drag her ass home.

Brandon had told me not do anything stupid. He was really starting to act like a bitch. I was regretting asking him to move in with me. The only benefit was in house dick.

I texted Mario that she had reached out to me and that she would be home tomorrow. His dumb ass had the nerve to tell me don't text him until she's actually home safe.

It took everything in me not to bust his shit. I hated that man with everything in me and I didn't know why. Honestly, I didn't care. The only reason I told him about my meeting with my sister was to draw him out of hiding.

See I did not know where he lived so I couldn't go handle him on my own. That shit bothered me like a muthafucka. I hated not being fully in control of any situation but I was trying to make this work in my favor.

Trying not to stress I went in to work and did something that I normally don't do. I talked to my co-workers. Turns out that they were some pretty cool and informative individuals.

The one chick that I sat next to everyday turned out to know Mario. I was so intrigued that she knew him and was a chatter box. She ran his life down to me and the news that I got from her had me beaming from ear to ear.

I no longer cared about seeing Renee's stupid ass. I had information that she didn't have and that could change both of our lives. This was too good. I thought about texting Brandon but decided not to.

For some reason he had been moving different. I couldn't figure out what he was doing because I didn't care but I knew it was something. Since I didn't know what it was I couldn't trust him.

I would have to keep this information to myself until the time was right to shut everybody up. For now I listened to the big mouth named Jeni talk about how she was the shit and who else she knew out in the streets.

It was times like this that I missed my sister. Her gullible side would play right along with people and make them think that she was interested and dumb. I didn't have that ability but I was surely trying to use it today.

Jeni had such a good time talking all day that she invited me to her house after work for a drink. I told her that I would love to but I had a previous engagement to attend.

She was cool and all but I was talking forever. But after work I did go to her house, she just didn't know it. I followed her to her house to see where she lived because she had mentioned that Mario frequented the area.

Just like she said he was there chilling with some other dudes on a porch just a few houses away from hers. He was an easy target. Maybe because he didn't expect that I would be bold enough to come for him.

I just laid low today and watched. Now that I knew where to find him I would definitely be back to handle this situation with him because like I said before no one talks to me like that and gets away with it.

After doing my steak out I went home to deal with whatever bullshit was awaiting me. I was feeling better than I had been in a while thanks to my informant Jeni.

"Hey Monae, how was work?" Asked Brandon

"It was actually a good day. How was being a home body for you?"

"It was therapeutic. I got a lot done around here."

As he said that I was walking into the kitchen and my jaw dropped. He had completely cleaned the kitchen. I'm talking walls, floors, backsplash, cabinet doors, and appliances were all sparkling.

"Next I'm going to sand the cabinets and give them a fresh coat of paint. So when will you be taking the car again?" He asked ignoring the tears running down my face

Once he noticed them he dropped his head and sadness replaced his happier look. I quickly grabbed his chin and lifted his head. I kissed him which was something I rarely did anymore.

It felt good to actually feel him kiss me back. I had missed his gentle yet firm touch. Lately everything had been forced, by me. I realized that my reaction was taken the wrong way and I had to correct it.

"Babe I love the kitchen."

His whole demeanor changed and a smile was now on his face.

"I thought I had fucked up." He said laughing

"No, I love what you did to the kitchen. Everything

looks one hundred times better and I know that our dad would have loved this."

"Yeah, I wanted to restore the house and preserve his memories for as long as I can."

Again I started crying.

"Yo, are you sure you aren't pregnant? You have been…"

I cut him off before he could finish. "A bitch lately?" I said

"Not my words but yes and very emotional." He added

I slumped down in a nearby chair and cried harder. As always Brandon was right by my side. I reached down and held his face then I spoke.

"Brandon I'm sorry for everything. I love you and can not take back the hurt that I caused you but please accept my apologies."

He kissed me and that let me know that he accepted my apology. But I wasn't finished yet. I decided in that split second to tell him what I had found out today. His eyes got big once I did and he immediately reached for his phone.

I jumped up to see who he was calling, it was Renee. But just like I thought she didn't answer. He turned to me and said "You need to tell her immediately!"

Chapter Fourteen

Renee

When I woke up this morning I had butterflies in my stomach something terrible. I was both excited and nervous as hell to meet with Monae today. Not just about the meeting but to execute my plan.

If all went well I would be well on my way to a stress free life. A life that I hoped to start over in a new city. I wanted to move away where no one knew me and I could have a fresh start.

But first I needed to see my sister. I got up to shower and I smelled the wonderful aroma of breakfast. Ashton had cooked bacon, eggs, hash browns, and sausage with a side of French toast.

I was blown away by his cooking skills. Not just because he could cook but he had skills. His food was always on point. I went into the bathroom and washed my face then brushed my teeth before heading into the kitchen.

He welcomed me to the table with a kiss and firm hug. It was like we had known each other for years and this was our normal. That kiss turned into a caressing. Caressing turned into undressing. Undressing turned into love making.

This man had some kind of hold on me and I was no longer fighting it. Ashton sat me on the kitchen counter and made love to me like I'd never felt before. Every touch was sensual and set my body on fire.

His hands traveled over every curve while paying close attention to those more sensitive areas. I moaned out loud calling his name over and over then I climaxed hard.

He wasn't finished yet. Ashton carried me to the bedroom where he laid me down and had his breakfast in bed. Yes, he devoured my pussy like it was his last meal.

I screamed his name as loud as I could. This shit felt so damn good. I needed this more than I needed breakfast. His head game was superb and of course his dick game was immaculate.

Now I was relaxed and ready for anything. We jumped in the shower together and I decided to show him that I was about that life too. I went down on my knees in the shower and began giving him head.

It was a sight to see. The water was running down on me while I sucked his dick. I showed him that I had skills too. My hair was all wet and stuck to my face but I didn't care.

I kept right on sucking until his babies shot down the drain. I loved watching this man nut. He would let out this sexy ass grunt that made me want more.

His head would roll back and that grunt would come from deep down then that nut would splash upon me. It was a great feeling. I loved seeing him satisfied by me.

But now we needed to get focused on the day ahead of us. He stepped out of the shower to allow me to cleanse myself. Ashton was so thoughtful and brought me so much peace.

Once I was out of the shower I collapsed onto the bed. Ashton saw this as an opportunity to take advantage of me. He got down on his knees and started sucking on my pussy.

I was in heaven as he licked on me and traced circles on my shit. I swear he wrote his name on it. But I didn't care what he did because it all felt so damn good.

After making me cum over and over again he finally let up. I sat up trying to catch my breath and regain my composure. It took me a minute because he knew how to please.

Now I was getting dressed while he washed his face again. He came back into the room and got dressed too. He looked so handsome. I was ready to get this over with so that I could focus on Ashton.

We left early so that we could get there before Monae. We wanted to see who else she brought or what tricks she would have up her sleeve. As we were headed to the park my phone started to blow up.

Brandon had been calling me nonstop since yesterday. I hadn't answered because I figured it was really all for Monae. She had called me first yesterday and I didn't answer then the calls started from Brandon.

I was in no mood for the bullshit so I ignored his calls and continued on to the park. No one had arrived yet so we found us a spot to watch from a distance without being seen.

This wasn't supposed to be anything other than a meet with my sister for information about what all has happened since I had been gone. But I was taking no chances.

That's why I had Ashton there and we were both strapped. I no longer trusted my sister so if she jumped stupid I would not hesitate to end her life. Yeah I thought about all of the times that she had been there for me but fuck that!

About thirty minutes went by before I noticed Brandon's car pull up. I didn't think she would allow him to come with her given how she had been treating him lately.

I slowly existed the vehicle being careful not to alert her to my location. I wanted to keep Ashton hidden and away from Monae. Not that I didn't like him but because I liked him. She hated every man that I talked to.

By the time she noticed me I was almost in her face. She jumped when she saw me and threw her guard up.

"So is that what we're doing?" I asked

"You scared the shit out of me. And what's with you?" She said referring to my attire

What I was wearing was completely out of character for me. I had on fitted black sweatpants, a fitted white tank top, sneakers, and my hair pulled into a ponytail. Even on my bad days I was never seen wearing shit like this.

But I had to be ready to move in case anything went off track. And I had a feeling that things would.

Chapter Fifteen

Monae

Renee came ready I see. She was dressed in casual wear that she never wore. She must have thought I was going to be on some stupid shit. I probably would have clowned had I not learned the information that I did from Jeni.

That little bit of information changed the game for me. I knew it would for Renee too but I didn't know if she was ready to hear me out about it. I stood there looking my sister from head to toe as she gave me the "rules" of the meeting.

Little sister was really trying to act grown on me. I laughed in my head at her attempt of taking control. But I had heard enough of her bullshit speech.

"Renee get to the point because I didn't come here for you to assert yourself and try to feel like a big girl. You said you wanted to talk."

"You agreed to this meeting so don't rush it and don't cut me off." Said Renee

"Look I don't give a fuck about none of this bullshit. You can go back to whatever hole you crawled out of with the bullshit." I snapped

"See that's your muthafuckin problem. You don't care about shit or nobody. All you care about is yourself. I'm trying to help both of us." Yelled Renee

"Help both of us? How the fuck you think you doing that?" I laughed

"I know Mario threatened you and I'm trying to take care of that situation for not just you, but me too."

"Girl I don't need you looking out for me but you might want to watch your back. I'm not the one sleeping with the enemy." I said smirking

"What the fuck does that mean?!" Renee said with a confused look on her face

"Just watch your back little sister." I said laughing and walking away

Her little meeting was pointless because she got no information from me and I didn't listen to anything that she had to say. As far as I was concerned after today

I no longer had a twin sister. I was a loner.

I walked away smiling the whole time. I was headed home to have the locks changed then off to work for me. She had completely wasted my time and I was in mood to keep playing with her.

No more would I be her protector if she was going to come at me like she had just done. Fuck her. She was now her own person and could take care of the bastard that wanted her dead on her own.

When I made it back home Brandon was pacing the floor. I had begged him to trust me and let me go alone. He had complied as a part of us rebuilding our relationship.

Now he wanted answers and I'm sure he didn't want the response that I was about to give him. He loved Renee like his own little sister so this was going to piss him off.

"So what happened? Where's Renee?" He asked frantically

"Probably still at the park where I left her stupid ass. She came at me wrong from the beginning so I left." I snapped at him

"What the fuck Monae!? For once can you just drop

the tuff shit? That's your fucking sister and she's in danger. Do you even fucking care?" Brandon yelled at me

"Obviously you care too fucking much! Since she's so grown and tuff now she can take care of herself. Fuck her." I stormed off to my room

I could hear him upstairs stomping around then the door slammed. I'm pretty sure that he was on his way to find Renee. I would've been concerned about his love for her but we had been together for five years and he was like family around here.

Just as I was about to call and curse him out for being on her defense I heard the floor creak upstairs. I laid my phone down on the bed and waited for him to come downstairs.

Two minutes went by before I got curious and angry. I stormed upstairs ready to give him a piece of my mind but was met by a fist instead. Night came early for me as everything went dark and I collapsed.

When I came to I couldn't hear or see anything. I could feel something tied around my eyes so I knew that I was blindfolded. My hands were bounded and so were my ankles. This couldn't be happening to me.

For the first time ever tears rolled down my face and

I welcomed them. I was experiencing a feeling that was not normal to me. Sadness crept up in me quick and it hit me hard.

When you're bound and can't see you use other senses more. My ears were picking up on all sounds around me. And what I was hearing didn't sound good for me.

Chapter Sixteen

Renee

I was so excited when the day started and now I was super pissed. Monae had shown up to the park with a shitty attitude and ruined what I had planned. Now I had to improvise.

Ashton waited until Monae left then approached me to see what happened. He came running up to me with anger all over his face. I was ready for him to chew me out as everyone always did but that wasn't the case.

"I knew her stuck up ass wouldn't fucking listen. Sorry but I hate your sister." He yelled as he kicked over a trash can

"It's okay babe. Calm down. If she doesn't want to face me here then I'll just have to dig a little deeper to find out what I need to know."

He walked up on me with a look in his eyes that I had never seen before. I didn't know what to expect. Then he picked me up as I wrapped my legs around him.

"Renee you are stronger than you know and I'm really proud of you. I've watched you mature in the short time that you've lived with me. I love you."

I didn't know what to do or say at that moment but thankfully my mouth spoke for me. I grabbed him by his face and kissed him before pulling away and saying "I love you too Ashton".

His eyes were still dark as hell but somehow had a twinkle to them. We kissed again but then I noticed another car in the distance like it was watching us. My eyes instantly got big as I saw David's car.

Why was his car here? And who was driving it? Why were they watching me and for how long had they been watching me? So many questions ran through my mind but this was no time for them.

I silenced my thoughts and concentrated on how to stay alive. I whispered in Ashton's ear about the suspicious vehicle then I dismounted. Once I was no longer in his arms he turned to face the car himself.

Ashton started to walk towards the car. I called out for him not to do it but he wasn't hearing anything that I was saying. He walked over to the car with urgency in his steps.

Before he could reach the car whomever it was sped off. I was relieved and pissed at the same time. I wanted to know who was behind this hit on my life yet I was thankful that nothing had popped off.

Against my better judgement I waited another half an hour at the park since I had one more person that was supposed to show. I had asked Mario to meet me here too but he never showed.

Me and Ashton decided to not stay at his house tonight just in case someone had followed us home. We checked into a hotel for the night and despite nothing going my way earlier it was pretty peaceful because I was with him.

I realized in that moment that I was falling for Ashton hard. This was the first time that I had fallen for someone based on pure feelings and not sex. It was a different type of feeling. He had my heart.

Even when I thought I loved David it was more like I loved the spotlight and sex. And with Mario I loved his matureness. But with Ashton I loved everything about him. He gave me butterflies.

It was then that I started to really brainstorm and

figure out what it was that I wanted in life. My gut still told me to leave the city but what else did I want. Spending this time with him made me realize that I wanted love.

That's all I had ever looked for in everyone but no one ever poured pure love into me so I would wild out. I was promiscuous because I was missing love. Now that I realized it there was no going back.

I walked up to Ashton and gave him the longest and most passionate kiss ever. He looked shocked at first but that look quickly turned to a smirk. I smirked back then stepped back to undress.

"Ashton I love you and I want to make a life with you." I said

"Renee I accept that invitation into your life and I welcome you into mine. You're such a sweet person and I would love the opportunity to grow with you." Ashton said smiling

He wrapped his long arms around me and embraced me. I followed that up with another deep kiss. The night was so special that you thought we would have had sex but we didn't.

It wasn't needed at this moment. Just holding each

other as we lay up and watched a movie was good enough. I just wanted to be safely in his arms. Before you knew it I had fallen asleep snuggled up under my favorite person.

Sadly I didn't stay asleep because my phone kept ringing. I awakened to see that it was Brandon blowing me up like he was crazy. I ignored his calls because I figured it was probably nothing urgent.

I wasn't concerned that anything had happened to Monae either because my twin senses weren't going crazy. So I returned my attention to my new man. I wanted to leave right now and start fresh but I was taught to never run from your problems. And I had already sort of done that.

This time tomorrow I would be ready to end some of my suffering for good.

Chapter Seventeen

Monae

I had been tied up and isolated for what seemed like days now. I honestly don't even know how long it had been. I was terrified though of what was to come. There were noises all around me so I knew that I wasn't alone.

Even though I could hear noises I didn't know how many people there were or anything. No one ever said anything around me, just movement. There sounded to be a grinder nearby and that terrified me even more.

I had never prayed so hard in my life until now. Every moment I was praying to God that I made it out of here alive. I swore to change my ways and my attitude towards others, whatever it took to get out of here.

Fear had my nerves rattled and adrenaline pumping so much so that I passed out. I had no clue how long I was out but when I came to I could tell that I had been moved.

Now I was sitting in a chair. Correction, I was tied to a chair. My legs and wrist were tied very securely to the chair so that I could not move in any way. The air felt cooler too. I had no clue if I was even in the same place.

Tears would have run down my cheeks but they were absorbed by the cloth over my eyes. This was like something out of a horror movie for me. It seemed like hours had gone by before I heard anything.

Unfortunately the sound that I heard was my own stomach growling. It was so loud that it startled me. I jumped from the shock and the pain associated with the rumbling.

After more time passed I heard a door open and a voice for the first time. The scary deep voice that belted out at me was one that I thought I recognized. Then he spoke again and I caught it.

"I said open your fucking mouth." I could tell he said this through clenched teeth.

"What for? Where am I?" I managed

"Bitch if you wanna ask questions I can let your ass starve!" He yelled at me

I did as I had been instructed to do although I was scared as hell for what was about to enter my mouth. Then I felt a spoon enter my mouth and tasted what seemed to be mashed potatoes.

Who the fuck feeds someone that's being held captive mashed potatoes? This idiot was crazy for real. Thankful that he was feeding me this odd choice of food but I was still scared shitless.

Was he feeding me to kill me? Would he be letting me go soon? Why was this man so bent on torturing me? So many more questions ran through my mind as he spoon fed me.

Finally the feeding stopped. An eerie feeling came across me as I realized he had left the room. I tried to move but I still couldn't. I was still tied down to this chair.

Then there was a blow to my chest. It took the wind out of me. I thought about ways to get free from the shackles. So I tried the infamous line "I have to use the restroom".

That didn't work either. I was smacked and this time the hand felt smaller than the last one. More feminine. My brain was all over the place. Who else was here torturing me?

I began to cry so much that the cloth on my eyes filled and began to let my tears fall. I knew that life as I knew it was over. I started to scream through my gagging hoping that someone would hear my cries but it was pointless.

Another blow shook me out of my thoughts but this time it was to my face. It hurt so much that I just knew that my jaw was broken on impact. Who had I hurt this bad?

Brandon was right. I had been a bitch and karma was coming for me quicker than I thought it would. And more brutal than I could have ever imagined.

Just then I heard heels clacking on the hard floor and now I was sure there was a woman here with this maniac. But who? She stopped somewhere in front of me and I could feel her presence.

Why could I feel her and not him? Did I know her? Was it Renee getting revenge on me for hurting her? I thought about the meeting that she wanted to have and how I shut her down without a fair shot.

"Renee if that's you I'm so sorry. I never meant to hurt you. I was just hurt myself and didn't know how to handle it." I sobbed

I heard a snicker behind my apology. Then I felt her bend down to my face. She was so close. I smelled the familiar aroma of Liz Taylor and cigarettes. It couldn't be who I thought it was.

"Too late for apologies Miss Monae." She said

"GiGi?" I cried even harder

There was no response.

"You have been a pain in the ass from day one little girl. First you kill my daughter then you move in and took over your father's life. It's because of you all that he took on extra shifts and had that accident. He wasn't scheduled to work that day." GiGi spoke

"That wasn't our fault! We miss him too." I yelled at her

"Like hell you do! You ungrateful misfit. I tried to teach you so much but you thought you knew every-thing. You couldn't wait to grow up and run the show. But Renee on the other hand learned very well. She was thankful for ever lesson and turned out to be a better person. Especially better than you."

I had nothing to say. She blamed me for everything. I

never realized that I had even hurt GiGi. I started shaking vigorously trying to break free from whatever was keeping me bounded.

But I wouldn't get the chance to. Another blow to my face took me out.

Chapter Eighteen

Renee

Waking up with Ashton after expressing my feelings to him yesterday felt so much better. It was like love was floating in the air. I eagerly sprung from the bed to wash my face and brush my teeth so that I could get back in bed with him.

While I was in the bathroom I checked my phone for missed calls and text messages. I had a few messages, all from Brandon. His messages were not priority to me but I checked them anyway.

Renee something is wrong. Monae didn't come home last night and I don't know where she could be.

AND MARIO IS DAVID'S COUSIN!! THAT'S WHO WANTS TO KILL YOU.

I dropped my phone reading that last line. The one that I spent time with was out to get me all this time. How could this be? Even more disturbing was the fact that Monae hadn't come home.

That was not normal for her. She would come home no matter how fucked up things were at home. I began to reminisce about the good times that me and Mario shared. I thought everything was going great.

He was such a gentleman. How could I not see the writing on the wall? Or was this just revenge for him and Monae arguing over my disappearance? I had no way of finding the answer to my questions and that hurt more than anything.

I was concerned about Monae but she had made it clear that she didn't need me. I had unfinished business to tend to. Brandon would have to file a missing person's report and fill me in later.

Since I had taken so long reading messages and panicking Ashton had awakened. He walked up to me hugging me from the back and kissed the back of my neck.

That was the sweetest and sexiest thing to me. I turned around and let my hand travel from his face down to his dick. I grabbed his morning erection and licked his lips before walking out of the bathroom.

I left him alone to take care of his hygiene but it didn't take him long once he turned to look out at me. I was laid out on the bed playing in my pussy. He hurried to finish brushing his teeth and washing his face only for me to mess it up again.

Ashton came back into the room with hunger in his eyes. He was eyeing me like I was breakfast, lunch, and dessert. I spread my legs a little wider for him to climb between. He did just that.

He licked me from my foot up to my wet and waiting pussy then he dove in head first. His skills were superb. This man took me out of my comfort zone. He flipped me over onto my stomach then brought my ass to his face.

I damn near squirted right away. He pulled me in close and started to lick me from front to back. Then he traveled back to the front. As he stopped and started sucking on my clitoris I began moaning and coming.

I was so fucking turned on that anything he did had me screaming and ready to blow. Oh my gosh this man was touching my soul with his tongue as he licked his name on my clit.

The water was flowing heavy with every lick and tug at my clitoris then he moved back to my ass and inserted his tongue. I lost it. Orgasm after orgasm came as I shook and cried out to him.

This man wasn't finished yet. He inserted his fingers into my pussy as he licked my ass then kissed a trail up my ass and down my back until his dick slid right in.

The feeling was out of this world. He had to hold me up because I went limp. My body was drained already and he was just now delivering the dick. Ashton sent tingles down my spine with every thrust.

Again the water started flowing. I was sure that I had no more left in me but it kept pouring out. Once I felt him flip me over again he then dragged me off the bed and picked me up. His strength surprised me.

He bounced me up and down on his dick while licking my nipples every time they bounced up by his mouth. I couldn't help but call out this man name over and over again.

Then his pounding got harder and deeper. I was loving his delivery. Then he came hard for me, inside of me. Although I had been promiscuous for some time now I had never let a man cum inside of me.

But this time I didn't even care. The dick down that I had just received was phenomenal. I laid there drained and gasping for air while he stood at the foot of the bed licking his lips at me.

I laughed at his confidence. It was one of the many things that I found attractive about him. No one would look at him and think that his nerdy looking ass was so fucking dynamite but I find him sexy as fuck.

He bent down and kissed me then smacked the little ass of mine that was exposed.

"Time to get busy baby."

I rolled out of the bed then said, "Yep, let's get this shit done bae".

Chapter Nineteen

Monae

Life was taking its toll on me. I just wanted to die at this point. Why was GiGi and Mario out to kill me? More importantly where were Brandon and Renee? Were they even looking for me?

GiGi had come back into the room. I could tell by the aroma in the air and the clicking of her heels. She was accompanied by the sound of chains and heavy items being dropped all around me.

"Time to set you free lil bitch." She said and a man laughed

I was so happy to hear that I would be going home. I had a lot to work on and I promised to God that I would actually do it. All I wanted was to see daylight again.

"I promise that I will change! I won't be the same Monae again. I have learned many lessons about how my attitude and actions affect others. Please let me go." I cried

"Oh no worries Monae. You will be free in no time so don't beg. Although it is cute coming from such a hard ass such as yourself." Said GiGi

"Me personally, I love to hear that trifling bitch beg." Mario said in a deep laugh

I wanted to curse his ugly ass out but that was part of the problem with my life. Apparently, I was too harsh on people. My short life had taught me a lot though. I knew that it would never be the same from here on out.

Sudden movement scared the shit out of me but not as much as what was happening. Someone had grabbed me by my hair while the other removed the restraints around my legs then arms.

This was a happy moment for me because I had been tied down to a chair for what seemed like weeks. I was happy to stretch my legs and to be going home. I wanted Brandon. I wanted my sister.

Regardless of my attitude or outlook on life I had to admit it. Renee was the peacemaker between the two of us. She was the one that used to bring me back down to earth when I flew off the handle. Renee was my handler.

I lost site of that and underestimated my sister because of her appearance and cool demeanor about things. I never understood how she let people get away with things no matter how small. Now I do.

To save yourself these problems that I'm in right now you have to turn the other cheek, as they say. I missed her. I'm sure that had I listened to her more in life I wouldn't be here in this situation. She would have saved me.

If only I had listened to her that day at the park. I could still be out there enjoying life and not sitting in a pool of my own bodily fluids. Suddenly I was shaken from my thoughts by a blow to my face.

Someone had punched me in my face with brass knuckles on. Wtf!? I guess I was to take an ass whooping before they let me go. The blow was so hard that I fell out of the chair.

That's when I realized that I was no longer tied down. That I could stand up. I tried to get up but that's when I felt a kick to my stomach then one to my face. I recognized the kick to my face as GiGi. Those heels did damage to my chin.

I couldn't believe that she hated me so much. The

woman that raised me and gave me so much advice. Maybe I should have listened some more. Then a stomp to my back took me out.

When I awakened, I was praying hard that I had been dumped somewhere far away from those psychos. I wasn't. I was still here with them. They were two monsters and I had to find a way out.

Still blindfolded I tried to feel my way out of there. I stood up as best as I could and felt my way around the room. I was feeling for doorknobs. I didn't find any doorknobs but I ran across some stairs. Freedom.

Then I heard him laugh again. "This bitch really thought she was gone get out of here so easy."

Just like that he punched me in the side of my face. I couldn't take many more blows. I was weak. I was sore. This was too much for me. I would never make it home in this condition.

Then it dawned on me. They never planned on letting me go home to Renee. I didn't know where Renee had been living but she had been living peacefully. It was me that they wanted all this time. They wanted to send me home to my mom and dad.

I scrambled to the stairs one more time. This time

I was crying my eyes out. They were still covered but my tears soaked the rag covering them. Panic had set in. I was in a bad situation. For the first time ever, I was alone and scared shitless.

I felt GiGi lock on to my hair while Mario picked me up by my legs. They laid me on what sounded like plastic. I was kicking, screaming, and crying. This couldn't be happening.

Mario held me down and delivered blow after blow to me. I was being beaten to death by a monster. He succeeded too. I died at the hands of Mario that day. I died after one of his blows to my head.

That didn't stop them though. They continued to beat me even after I died. For me it didn't matter. I had died behind my own actions. I had left my sister in this cruel world. I had died alone.

That's what hurt me the most.

Chapter Twenty

Renee

My first stop was to my house. Or my old house as I should say because I had no plans on coming back. My new living quarters were with Ashton. I tried opening the door with my key but it wouldn't budge.

I knocked on the door and after not getting a response I called Brandon. He answered right away.

"Sis, what's up? You find Monae?" He said franticly into the phone

"No, I haven't. I'm at the house trying to get in. Why doesn't my key work?" I questioned him

"Monae had the locks changed for safety reasons."

I could tell that he was lying. I wanted to call him out on it but now was not the time to turn into petty Betty so I left it alone.

"Yeah okay. Well I'm here trying to find out what's

going on?"

"I'll be there in a minute Sis." And he hung up

Regardless of what my sister had going on I knew that Brandon wasn't a part of it. He genuinely cared about her evil ass. Besides the concern in his voice told me that he had not been to sleep since she didn't come home.

I felt sorry for him at times but then again he helped to bring out the best of both worlds with Monae. He saw the softer side but everyone else got the harder side from her. He was a gift and a curse.

Ashton and I got back in the car to wait for him. It seemed so quiet around here. Like you knew something bad was about to happen. Like in the horror movies. I just wanted to get this day over with already.

It didn't take Brandon long to get to the house. It never did though. For one he drove like a bat out of hell. Secondly, he never wanted to keep us waiting for him. It's been that way for years.

When Brandon arrived he looked like he had been through the ringer. This man couldn't have slept or eaten. He looked like shit. I couldn't do anything but hug him because he cared about my sister and it really showed.

He hugged me back with the tightest hug ever. The hurt was evident. We followed his lead into the house and I was in shock. It looked like shit too. I turned to him in shock.

"What the hell happened? You didn't tell me she was in this kind of trouble." I cried out

"I don't know if she is or isn't. I did this to the house when she didn't wasn't home and wasn't answering her phone. I went a little crazy before I went looking for her."

"Brandon have you thought that maybe she took off on her on?"

"Nope. She wouldn't do that. We had just had an argument about you when she stormed down to her room. I left because I was pissed. When I came home she wasn't here but all of her stuff is still here."

"So, what the fuck happened? Why were you two arguing about me?" I inquired

"I told her that she was wrong for not listening to you and that she should have told you about Mario. That's why I ended up texting it to you in hopes that you would see it."

"How did you figure this out?" Asked Ashton

"Monae did. She worked with a girl that spoon fed her information about Mario. She had no clue that you all knew him or was looking for him."

Brandon broke down crying. "I just want my baby back. We need to go find this nigga because I'm sure he has something to do with it."

"I'm sure she's okay because my twin senses aren't going crazy. We'll find her big brother." I hugged him tight and let him cry it out

Once we had all of our emotions out of the way we all jumped into our cars to go looking for Monae. Of course the first stop was Mario's place. He wasn't there. I should have known that it wouldn't be that easy to track him down.

We left and just went riding around looking for her or him. I kept my eyes open for signals. Anything that I thought might have been a sign from Monae I was on it. We hit the streets asking people if they had seen her and it was like she just vanished into thin air.

By the end of the night we were worn out. We decided to call it a night and start fresh in the morning at Mario's house. But on the ride home I felt different than when we originally set out in search of my sister.

I felt at peace. Like Monae was at peace. Tranquility set in and that scared me. Why was I feeling so light? I had to find Mario. I needed to find my sister. These loose ends needed to be tied up quickly.

Chapter Twenty-One

(A Voice from Beyond)

They had killed me and left me on the cold floor, carefree. These monsters had actually went and ordered food while I laid on this tarp waiting for them to come back.

Eventually they did but by now there was no sunlight anywhere in sight. It was the middle of the night when all things and people were asleep. The dark skies were their cover.

They wrapped me in the tarp that I was laying on and carried me out to the trunk of a car. Even in spirit this was hard on me. I watched them load my lifeless body away then drive off.

The car stopped at a secluded field about an hour away from the city. There was a lake not far from where the car stopped. I guess the water was about to become my final resting place.

Mario tied string to my legs then wrapped my legs together. He used those ropes to drag me through the field and over to the lake. There GiGi was waiting with some cinder blocks to weigh me down.

GiGi tied the blocks to the end of the ropes on my legs. Next, Mario the monster rolled me into the lake until I started to sink. They didn't stick around to find out if I went all the way down to the bottom. As long as I was unseen they were happy. The two of them drove back home as if nothing had happened. Crazy thing is they still didn't care for each other. Their love of hate for me brought them together.

Both of them returned to the house to clean up the mess that they left behind. Blood splatter was everywhere. A pool of my urine was collected on the floor underneath where I was seated.

GiGi cleaned the car while he got started on the basement. It was a mess in there but the trunk was surprisingly clean. No blood had dripped in the trunk of the car. They were careful with that because it was a rental.

After cleaning the basement of whatever building they were in it was time to go their separate ways. They said nothing to each other as they exited the building. Crazy how the hate for one person can bring two people together.

But things wouldn't go so well for either of them in life. They would definitely get a dose of karma before it was too late. For now they were in the clear.

GiGi returned home and gathered a few of her belongings. With Renee in the wind and me gone fishing there was no reason for her to stick around. Upon her return home she didn't see Brandon so she figured she was good.

Thankfully Brandon was out of sight but he saw her return home. He also saw Mario pull up in a new car then get out to talk to her. The two looked like they were exchanging words.

GiGi handed him some money then he left just as quickly as he pulled up. Brandon didn't blow his cover but with him knowing that Mario wanted to do harm to us why would she be talking to him? And giving him money?

This made Brandon inferior. The woman that raised them and taught them to always watch the company you keep was dancing with the devil. He knew at that moment that GiGi wasn't the person that she claimed to be.

Now things started to make sense to him. She was never around when things went down and she hadn't even checked in recently to express concern about what happened. She was a foul bitch.

Brandon instantly grew concerned for my whereabouts and Renee's. He reached for his phone and called her. He got no answer. This wasn't the time to go M.I.A. He began to panic.

He ran across the street to see if Renee was there but he got no answer. Ashton's car was not there and Brandon didn't have his number to call him. He felt hopeless. His world was falling apart and there was nothing that he could do about.

He tried calling Renee one more time hoping that she would answer. He prayed as the phone rang but still no answer. Then his phone rang back. It was Renee.

"Sis, where y'all at?" He said eagerly

"We're on our way to Mario's. Meet us there."

That was all that he needed to hear.

Chapter Twenty-Two

Renee

We had taken a nap to regain some of our energy. Well at least I took a nap. I don't think Ashton slept. Once I got up he sat straight up in the bed staring at me in silence. He was waiting on my move.

I got up and headed into the bathroom. Once I got to the door of the bathroom I turned around and motioned for him to come join me. I proceeded to wash my face and brush my teeth while he stood behind me patiently waiting.

Ashton had turned the shower on so after I was finished he picked me up and whisked me into the shower. I was terrified that he would drop me so he put me down and bent me over instead.

That was the best thing ever. The water running down my body as he entered me was ecstasy. I was had one hand on the edge of the tub and one braced against the shower wall for balance.

Ashton was going hard behind me like our lives were depending on it. Hard and deep strokes back to back. I was losing my mind with every thrust. This man was delivering the dick.

As I felt my climax rising, I started screaming to him "Go harder daddy! Harder!"

He grunted then let out one hell of a nut. As he filled me up with his love I released my love onto him. It felt so good that I did not want to break our connection. He must have felt the same way because he didn't move either.

The sound of a phone ringing broke us apart, well sort of. He finally pulled himself out me then turned me around and started kissing me. It was so romantic standing there in the shower sharing our love for each other.

We finally made our way out of the shower. Without seeing who was calling we got dressed because we had business to take care of. Once I was dressed I sat there at the foot of the bed listening to the phone ring again.

I guess it was my phone that had been ringing because Ashton handed it to me but by the time I answered it the phone had stopped. I saw that it was Brandon and I quickly returned the call hoping that he had information on my sister.

He didn't say anything but the urgency in his voice scared me. Brandon said that he would meet us at Mario's house so that we could all get this over with. It was time.

I rode in silence because I was still bothered by the feeling I had the night before. Where was Monae? Why had I gotten that feeling? I prayed that she was okay and waiting for me to rescue her.

We arrived at Mario's house and surprisingly he was at home. This was the golden moment for us. Brandon decided that he would go knock on the door. It was a good distraction for me and Ashton to go around back and break in.

Yeah we all could have just shown up at the front door for answers but we knew that we wouldn't get the truth. So Brandon got himself in place while Ashton and I went around back.

Once we knew that Mario had opened the door for Brandon we snuck in through the patio door. I knew that he always kept that door unlocked for whatever reason.

I texted Brandon that the patio door was open then we waited for Mario to approach us. Mario didn't talk long to Brandon but at least he did open the door.

"What do you want?" Said Mario

"I know you don't give a fuck but have you seen Monae or Renee? I haven't seen them in a while."

"Nah if I had they would've come back to you crying and bloody."

"Yeah okay. Don't underestimate me because I'm not the one. Fucking with my girls will get you fucked up." Brandon said moving closer to Mario

Mario just laughed and slammed the door in Brandon's face. I was glad because I didn't want Brandon out there fighting. Everything that we were going to do would be done in the house.

Brandon played it off as if he was walking to his car but he headed around back when Mario walked away from the window. It was time. We had been waiting in the kitchen with weapons in hand.

I didn't care about giving him a chance to say anything. He wanted to harm me and he threatened my sister so he had to go. Before he made it to the kitchen he placed a call.

"You need to take care of that nosey ass boyfriend of hers. He just came by my house questioning me about that one." He huffed into the phone

We couldn't hear the other person's voice but I had feeling that Brandon knew something because he got a weird look on his face. He looked like he had seen a ghost.

Chapter Twenty-Three

(A Voice From Beyond)

While they were all off with their own agendas I was floating in the lake about to rise again as I have so many times in life. Today was a busy day at the lake because it was good weather for fishing.

There were so many small groups out today. Men out teaching their son's to fish or just bonding at the lake. There was a small group of older men just hanging out enjoying the morning air.

The lake was alive early this morning. As one of the fishermen casted his line it started to sink. On its way to the bottom it snagged on something. That something was my hair.

His hook had tangled in my hair as he tugged gently trying to bait the fish. The weight from my body caused him to think that he had caught a big fish. He started to reel in.

It was a happy and sad day for me. I didn't stay in the water long so that was good but to be found dead was heartbreaking. The lake was disturbed by the screams of a young boy who witnessed the reel in.

Police lights and sirens filled the peace that once was the lake environment. People were all standing around looking on in shock. It was like something out of a movie.

The police eventually cleared the area so that they could successfully pull me from the lake and send a dive team in to recover any evidence that might have drifted away from my body.

I was alone in this new world watching as so much unfolded in the world that I took for granted. The community was shaken and they didn't even know the full story of what happened yet.

In this city news traveled fast so it would only be a short time before Renee found out what happened. I knew this would devastate her and Brandon. He wouldn't know what to do. I knew he loved me more than a little.

The investigating crew stayed at the lake until late that night/early morning. When they were finished they carried me to my new home, the city morgue. I would sit there for a total of 45 days.

It hurt to feel so alone and isolated. But I guess I had done that to myself before I died and I just hadn't realized it. I had pushed everyone away with my attitude and now I paying for it.

After forty days in the morgue Renee finally started to look for me. She had been so down and heartbroken that I couldn't blame her for not finding me sooner. At least she did it.

Renee was talking to someone who asked about me and if Renee had any new information. Of course she didn't so the girl says "That's too bad. That's just like that case where they pulled that girl out of the lake a month ago. No one said anything more about it."

That made Renee's hair stand up on her arms. Why hadn't she heard about this? And it made the news too? So she went to investigate the lake and pulled up the article on her phone.

It was the description that did it for her. Renee rushed down to the police station inquiring about the girl found in the lake. The officer gave her the details then showed her a picture.

She broke down in the middle of the lobby. Thankfully Ashton was by her side to catch her as she fell to the floor screaming and crying. After filling out the necessary paperwork she got to take my ashes home with her.

This furthermore made her depressed. I don't believe she would have made it if it wasn't for Ashton being in her life. I was all that she had. Or at least I was until I pushed her away.

That guilt of my murder weighed heavy on her heart. I could still feel it. I could still sense when she wasn't herself. I guess I just wanted to still be close to my sister too. And she was still holding me close to her heart.

It took Renee another month to get her mind right and return to some of her normal activities. Ashton never left her side. He was proving to be the best boyfriend that she ever had. And there were a few.

Although I would never be able to tell her that I was proud of her and that I would always be with her to protect her, I knew she felt it. Our twin bond couldn't be broken. Not even in death.

Chapter Twenty-Four

Renee

As we were still standing in the kitchen waiting on Mario bitch ass to come around the corner Brandon lost it. He walked out into the dining room presenting himself for Mario.

We stood back to see what action Mario would take. It didn't matter because Brandon didn't give him enough time to draw a weapon. He rushed Mario and tackled him like he played in the NFL.

They started fighting then we rushed over to watch. He didn't need help so we stood back waiting. Then the perfect opportunity presented itself. As Brandon climbed to his feet I struck Mario with a kick to the head.

That dazed him long enough for Brandon to stand and regain his composure. Ashton kicked the leg of the dining room chair and broke it then he struck Mario with it repeatedly.

We all stood there beating this man until Brandon finally said stop. We stood there confused and looking at him. Then that's when I saw the blood pouring from his neck.

Sometime during the fight Brandon had slit Mario's throat. I wanted to ask him about my sister but now I'll never get the chance. I was pissed at Brandon.

"Why would you kill him before I could talk to him?!" I yelled

"Oh so you thought because you fucked him that he was going to answer you and treat you better?" Brandon shot back

I thought about it for a minute. I was still pissed but he had a point.

"Still no one got a chance to see where Monae is."

"I know you don't want to hear this but I believe she's already gone. I saw him pull up to GiGi's house the other day and they argued about something then she gave him something and he left."

"That doesn't mean that my sister is gone idiot!" I screamed at him

"Baby, what he's saying is that's who he placed the call too when we got here. GiGi has something to do with this shit too." Said Ashton in his cool and calm fashion

"Exactly! So you weren't getting no information out of him." Exclaimed Brandon

"So what do we do with him?" Asked Ashton

"Shit leave that nigga stinking right here."

I nodded my head in agreeance. We all looked at each other and without saying a word we walked towards the back door. We left without ever talking about Mario again. He no longer existed.

Brandon followed us back to the hotel so that everyone could get cleaned up before being seen in public. After we all got ourselves together we headed back to my dad's house.

It was a quiet day. Almost eerily quiet. We all went inside of the house quickly and quietly. We were trying to get in without being seen by GiGi. I noticed that she had bags packed and sitting by the door as I caught a glimpse into her living room window.

Now I definitely knew that she had something to do

with Monae's disappearance. Why else would she be packing up to leave so quick and without telling us? I had to catch her before she left. She had to pay too.

I decided to play my innocent girl role and just go to her house. I knocked on the door and she answered instantly. She didn't let me in though. I knew something was up at that point.

"Have you seen Monae? I was supposed to meet her but she never showed." I said sounding as scared as possible

"Nah I haven't seen her in a few days. I figured she was working all of the time."

She lied right to my face. I let her see a few tears roll down my face just to shake her up more. It worked like a charm. This was the first time that I saw any fear on GiGi.

Her eyes widened and she looked sad. I knew right then and there that she knew more than what she was saying. So I kicked her so hard in the stomach that she went flying backwards.

I closed the door behind me and went to work on GiGi. Rage set in and I swear that I saw my sister standing back watching with a smile on her face. This was for her.

GiGi tried to get her footing but I tripped her and slammed her face into the floor repeatedly. When I got tired of doing that I flipped her over and beat the shit out of her.

Again I swear I heard Monae talk to me. I heard the faint sound of her voice saying "Sis I love you". That only made me madder. I began crying and throwing blow after blow to GiGi's face.

I didn't stop until the rage turned to hurt. Even then I got up and picked up a big flower pot that she had and I dropped it on her head. Blood splattered everywhere. I didn't care. I finally felt peace.

I left her right there and went back next door. When I entered both Brandon and Ashton jumped up screaming. I reassured them that it wasn't my blood then I collapsed. That's all that I remember.

Chapter Twenty-Five

Renee

I woke up cleaned and in bed at home with Ashton. He said that Brandon had called the police saying that he found GiGi dead. When asked who could have done it Brandon told them whoever was responsible for Monae's disappearance.

They bought it and left him alone. Ashton said that they came looking for me but I was asleep already. He told the police that I barely left bed because of my sisters abduction.

I would eventually talk to the police. After weeks of putting up flyers and searching for Monae someone mentioned something that shook my core. I followed the words of this individual to the police station.

The officers there thought I was crazy but I didn't leave until I got answers. As it turns out my sister was murdered over a month ago. It was an unsolved mur-

der and because no one claimed her body she was cre-
mated.

I picked up the ashes and took my sister home. That was the best and worst day for me. I spent so much time in the bathroom vomiting my life away. My twin, my sister, my heart, my love was gone.

It took some time for me to accept it and start healing but Ashton never left my side. He was my everything. I had no one left and had hit rock bottom but he slowly built me back up. I loved him for that.

Ashton helped me get dressed this morning. My plan was to go to the lake and have a private memorial for Monae. I just wanted to say goodbye to her at the last place she was seen.

It was a peaceful memorial. I cried and said my apologies for not being there for her when she needed me. It felt like she was speaking to me because I felt a little better by the end of the night.

We decided that staying here was too much for me. Ashton thought it would be a good idea to move out of state. Missouri had been my home all of my life but we were now set out to find a new home.

Brandon also decided to pack up and head out of Missouri too. Although Brandon was like a brother to me, we were parting ways. I was going to start my life with Ashton and hopefully start a family soon.

Our first stop was just for fun. We went to the Lincoln Museum in Springfield, Illinois. It was one of my favorite places to visit. It was here that my life changed forever.

Ashton waited until we were in front of a nice crowd then he stopped me. He looked me right in my eyes and dropped down on one knee. Instantly I began to cry. This couldn't be happening.

"Renee I love you with all of my heart and I told you that I want you in my life forever. I want to be there every step of the way as you continue to grow into the beautiful woman that you are becoming. Will you marry me Renee?"

I began to cry even more hysterically. Everyone was watching us and waiting on my answer. Through tear filled eyes and barely audible words I answered.

"Yes! Of course I want to start a life with you. I love you Ashton."

We got a huge round of applause from the crowd. It was such a magical moment for me. This would be a memory that I would cherish forever. Not just because he proposed but at the museum of all places.

I was slowly getting back to myself. Maybe an even better version of myself. I honestly think that he was helping me to become that better woman too. We continued to travel and just enjoy life together.

Eventually we would settle down in a small town called Thorton. It was a small town down south where the winters were still warm yet the summers were sunny and full of fun.

Life was different for me without my sister but I knew that she would be happy for me. She hated that I talked to so many guys so to see me settling down would make her day.

And although she didn't have the chance to get to know Ashton I'm sure she would have loved him. She was hard on the guys in my life but that's because they were only using me. Ashton was different.

The more I thought about life with this man the more I was ready for that big day. I lost a lot in life but this was my chance to turn things around for the better. I wouldn't let this opportunity pass me by. This was my moment and I was going to make my dad, sister, and even my mom proud of me.

About The Author

Yanee Brinks

Yanee Brinks was born in Saint Louis, MO in August of 1985. In the late 2000's I became a wife to an amazing man and shortly thereafter we became the parents of four wonderful children.

Being born an only child let the mind roam often and an active imagination was soon born. After finding comfort in reading and falling in love with books I began to let my own words flow on paper starting with poems and short stories.

I self published my first novel, Sip, Read & Fantasize: Short Reads for the Adult Minds, in September of 2019. That was followed up by the release of the three part novel Birth of a Side Chick in December of 2019, Death of a Side Chick in January of 2020, and Love, Lies, & Murderous Affairs in July of 2020.

I love reading and writing so I will deliver you more

books! Stay tuned.

Make sure to follow me for new releases!

Books In This Series

Monae & Renee

Monae & Renee: A Tale Of Two Sisters

Monae and Renee are sisters like no other. Besides being born twins they are best friends and let nothing nor no one come between them. And they do mean no one. With a mom in the streets and a father that often gets pushed away they have only each other.

So with a rocky childhood they were forced to grow up fast and had to learn to survive in the streets. But when you live in the streets life throws you plenty of test and obstacles. Their first obstacle coming very early in life taught them just how close they were and how much closer they would become in life.

Determined to make it in the gritty world these sisters will do anything see one another thrive. Together they can do it but can they stand up to the mean streets and each other when one chooses a different lifestyle?

Books By This Author

Ghetto Girls Handbook

A book that touches the subject of being GHETTO!! Being ghetto isn't just a black thing either so put that thought to the side.

This humorous book will talk about all of the things that you know you shouldn't be doing but you do them anyway. Yeah we're all guilty of some not so good behavior but some of us have made it a way of life. That needs to change and hopefully this book can give you some insight as to what those things are that you need to adjust. This book will also help you understand why you need to adjust your way of life.

From clothes, to speech, to children, and self love we talk about it all.

Falling For The Wrong One

Gemini Wilks was born an only child so she was no

stranger to being a loner especially when you come from a family of money. But Gemini takes a chance and becomes friends with an outgoing young lady name Mya Brooks. They are best friends and Mya treats Gemini like family. So does Mya's family.

But when Mya introduces Gemini to two of her male friends from the neighborhood things take a bad turn. Lies are told and secrets get revealed turning everyone's life upside down. Will their friendship hold up through these tough times? Or will someone pay the ultimate price?

Birth Of A Side Chick

Jalyn feels that she was born to be great and do great things. So far that is true. But the one thing that she wants the most doesn't seem to be in her reach and that is her dream guy. She buries herself in her work and does an amazing job at it but outside of that all she has is her friend McKenzie.

McKenzie aka Mac has had her own relationship issues and is ready to settle down herself. Feeling that it's time for a change Jalyn and McKenzie decide to put an end to bad relationships. That's when everything changes for both women.

A secret shared changed Jalyn's life but was it for the best? And can McKenzie finally land Mr. Right? Can the stars align for both friends to find their happily ever after? Life is never that simple…

Death Of A Side Chick

The gang is back in part two of the Side Chick Series!

After being a side chick to Malik and experiencing so much heartache Jalyn has finally found a love of her own. Her ex LaTrei has returned and he's not letting go this time. He's even proposed but can they both shake the demons that follow them in order to make it work?

McKenzie has also found a love of her own. One being her business venture and the other being Cordell. They have both experienced life changing situations but her and Cordell are going strong and starting a family together. He's determined to change for the sake of starting a family but old habits die hard.

Can they keep the love alive in their current relationships or will their lives come crashing down around them?

Love, Lies, & Murderous Affairs

After marrying the man of her dreams Jalyn's life was going good. That is until she finds out that her husband is entertaining other women in his free time. Feeling hurt and betrayed sends her mind into a dark place that causes her to act out of character. Jalyn has giving him all of her love, a child, and a wonderful life so what is it that he's missing.

LaTrei knows that he has a good woman but can't keep himself focused on just her so trouble in paradise is brewing. He loves Jalyn and doesn't want to lose her so what is he to do? He just can't help himself. Well LaTrei has one affair that will help them find the perfect solution to this problem.

With love, lies, and numerous affairs troubling this power couple can they save the love that they have for one another? Or will their love not be enough to end LaTrei's wondering eyes? Or will their worlds be turned upside down when a death falls at their doorstep.

Sip, Read, & Fantasize: Short Reads For The Adult Mind

Just want a quick read? Want to get lost in the world of erotica? Then let these short stories carry you away as you Sip, Read, & Fantasize. These short love stories are guaranteed to keep you interested and fantasizing about your own love life. So grab your drink and settle down for a little adult read!

Naughty Girl Poems

This collection of poems is for the adults only! These

edgy urban poems are sure to get your fire burning. So sit back, relax, and let my these naughty poems stimulate your mind.

Follow Me

www.Facebook.com/YaneeBrinks

www.Instagram.com/YaneeBrinks

https://Amazon.com/Author/Yaneebrinks

www.ingramcontent.com/pod-product-compliance
Lightning Source LLC
Chambersburg PA
CBHW051824180726
47991CB00028B/597